Scritch! Scratch!

Meg Caraher

Illustrated by Pat Reynolds

Supa DooPers

sundance
A Haights Cross Communications Company

Published by
Sundance Publishing
P.O. Box 1326
234 Taylor Street
Littleton, MA 01460
800-343-8204
www.sundancepub.com

Copyright © text Meg Caraher
Copyright © illustrations Pat Reynolds
Project commissioned and managed by
Lorraine Bambrough-Kelly, The Writer's Style
Designed by Cath Lindsey/design rescue

First published 1999 by
Addison Wesley Longman Australia Pty Limited
95 Coventry Street
South Melbourne 3205 Australia
Exclusive United States Distribution: Sundance Publishing

ISBN 0-7608-6631-7

Printed in Canada

Contents

For Ginny Stockton, my American mom.
Thank you for twenty years of love, across the
miles. M.C.

Acknowledgment
My gratitude goes to Jennifer Cooper, Education Officer for The Asthma Foundation of South Australia Inc., for her feedback and technical advice.

CHAPTER I

Stop Scratching

Scritch. Scratch.

"Oh, no! Miguel's got the itches again," Nina whispered. She moved to the far end of the couch to get away from her brother.

"Stop it! Stop scratching. I can't stand that scraping sound. Nails on skin. Yuck!" said Nina, gritting her teeth.

Miguel laughed and kept scratching.

"Can't stop, Nina. Scratching's my life," teased Miguel.

"Stop scratching, Miguel," said his older sister, Marta, looking up from her homework. "Those horrible red lumps are already breaking out on your arm."

"You've been to Josh's house, haven't you? Even though Mom said you're not to go there, you went," said Nina. "*And* you patted the cat, didn't you, Miguel?"

"Worse than that," said Miguel, starting to look miserable. He reached behind his knee to scratch.

Nina noticed that his eyes were bloodshot. Soon his eyelids would blow up and look like two red party balloons. "Worse?" asked Nina.

CHAPTER 2

Medicine Room

"Josh's cat had kittens. And Josh let me hold them . . . all of them," muttered Miguel.

"For a ten-year-old kid, you can be pretty stupid," said Nina. She got up to find his cream.

"For a twelve-year-old kid, you can be pretty mean, Nina," said Marta as Nina left the room.

"And I've told you before—don't call me stupid!" shouted Miguel, scratching. He was surrounded by a cloud of bits of skin.

Most families had a medicine chest. The Barco family had a medicine *room*. Every Barco, except Nina, had lots of allergies.

It seemed that Nina only came into this room to get things for other people. Just as Nina reached out her hand for the tube of Miguel's cream, she heard the door slam shut behind her.

Then she heard the rattle of the key
turning in the lock. Nina raced to the door.
Too late. She was locked in!

CHAPTER 3

Prisoner

"Let me out! What's going on?" shouted Nina. She pulled on the door handle.

Her parents locked the medicine room door for safety whenever other kids came over.

From the other side of the door came a laugh that she knew well.

"You shouldn't have called me stupid," called Miguel.

Nina yelled back, "Open the door, now! Open the door, you little . . ."

"Not until you sign a paper swearing I'm not stupid," replied Miguel.

A sheet of paper and a pen were pushed under the door.

"You're an even bigger fool than I thought," said Nina scornfully.

She tore the paper into little pieces and pushed them back under the door. She heard Miguel walk away, whistling.

That was it. She was a prisoner!

CHAPTER 4

Losing It

As far as allergy sufferers went, there was something for everyone in the Barco's medicine room. Nina's mom was allergic to pollen and bee stings.

Marta had severe asthma. She always got hay fever in the spring. And she was allergic to penicillin.

Miguel's skin was always itching. He was allergic to anything that meowed, squeaked, or barked—anything on four legs, really.

Dad was allergic to lots of different foods. He couldn't eat strawberries or eggs. And he had to be careful about eating different kinds of shellfish and nuts.

"My family is a twenty-first-century mess," muttered Nina to herself.

The windows in the medicine room were up high in the wall.

"This really is like being locked in a cell," cried Nina, looking around the room for something to climb on.

Nina looked at all the bottles of pills, tubes and jars of cream, and medical equipment. Nina saw the crutches Mom had used after a bee had stung her on the foot. She'd needed them because even after she'd come home from the hospital, her foot was still the size of a basketball.

The crutches! Nina leaned them against the wall. She tried to use them to climb up and open the window. As she twisted the window lock, one of the crutches slipped. Down she went.

"I'm losing it! I'm really losing it!" yelled Nina. She rushed to the door to bang on it, when it suddenly opened!

CHAPTER 5

Shocked

"Nina! Come out of there. Miguel, how could you lock this door without telling anyone? What if Marta had needed a refill for her inhaler and couldn't get it?" said Nina's mother.

Nina shook her head in disbelief. Not a word of concern for her, the person locked in. Her mother opened a tube of cream and started dabbing Miguel's angry rash.

"Really, Miguel, don't ever do that again," Mom said. She didn't notice that Nina's face had turned as red as Miguel's rash.

"Yeah, well, I'm having an allergic reaction of my own, Mom!" Nina shouted, unable to stop herself. "I'm allergic to my *brother!* I was the poor sucker he locked in. And you haven't asked me if I'm OK. You haven't even told him to say he's sorry."

"Miguel's sorry, aren't you, Miguel? Look, Nina, I haven't got time for this. Your father's waiting in the living room for everyone. We've made a big decision, and we want to tell you kids about it," said Mom. She screwed the lid back on the tube.

"Once again, Nina gets the brush-off," Nina whispered bitterly.

It just wasn't fair. She'd gotten a bad deal—middle child, no allergies. In the Barco family, an allergy meant attention. You never even got a second glance unless you were having a good scratch. An allergic reaction meant days off from school, snuggled up on the couch watching TV.

And it meant . . . presents. Marta and Miguel actually got presents for being such good allergy sufferers!

"I bet I'm adopted," grumbled Nina, making her way to the living room. "I'm not from the same gene pool. I'm so healthy, it stinks. And I'm badly short of presents."

But Nina had presents coming her way, only not the kind of presents she wanted. They were good-bye presents!

CHAPTER 6

#

"Moving? Where? Why? Do we have to?" cried Nina.

Her parents explained to the children that they had decided the family should move to the country.

Dad said, "If we leave the city and move to the country, Marta's asthma problem might lessen. There's just too much dust in the air around here."

"And Miguel is having all sorts of strange little difficulties," added Mom. "We think that he's allergic to life in the city."

"Well, can't we just put him in a bubble suit or something?" demanded Nina.

Within a few short months, Nina found herself relocated to Heysville, or Hicksville, as she called it.

Away from the city, everyone's allergies seemed better, except Mom found out that she was allergic to sword grass.

But Nina missed her friends and hadn't made many new ones. She was lonely.

One day, Nina and Marta were invited to an overnight at Amy's farm. Amy Bergner was one of the most popular girls at the small country school.

"This is big, Marta," said Nina, waving the invitation at her sister. "This could mean we're in."

"Hey, not so fast," said Mom, frowning. She read the invitation and then shook her head.

"I'm afraid you'll have to say no, girls. I can't have Marta on a farm. Think of all that fur, feathers, hay, and straw. My goodness, she'd have the asthma attack of the century!"

"Yes, but, Mom, what about me?" squeaked Nina. "Couldn't I go? I'm not allergic to anything. Remember *me?*"

CHAPTER 7

The Sleepover

"Nina, this is such a cool birthday present. Thanks," said Amy, looking at the cover of the CD.

Nina smiled and munched on some chips. The other girls made approving noises, and Nina felt happy. She liked these girls, and she could tell that they felt the same about her. At last—friends!

"Have you ever slept in a hay shed before,
Nina?" asked Greta, one of Amy's friends.
She had hair like Nina's—short, thick, and
curly.

"Never. Why?" asked Nina.

"Amy's older brother, Chris, has dared us to sleep the whole night out there," laughed Greta.

"He thinks we'll chicken out because it's cold out there at night. But we'll show him," said Amy.

As they settled into their sleeping bags between hay bales, talking seemed to help keep out the cold. But as it got later, the fun of sleeping in the hay shed wore off. Before very long, two of the girls went back to the house.

"Well, I'm staying," announced Amy, yawning sleepily.

"Me, too. I'm not cold at all," said Greta.

"I'm staying, too. This is the chance of a lifetime for me," giggled Nina. "Sleeping in a hay shed! If my mom knew, she'd have a fit! I come from the *most* allergic family that ever lived."

"What are you allergic to?" asked Greta.

"Nothing. I'm the odd one out in my family! I could walk around all day with a beehive sitting on my head. I could eat fresh strawberries dipped in penicillin. I could play with every animal on your farm, Amy, and I wouldn't sneeze, swell up, or scratch anywhere!" laughed Nina.

Soon Amy fell asleep. In between whispering to Greta, Nina found herself nodding off.

The next time she opened her eyes, she could only make out one other shape. It was Greta. Everyone else had gone inside. Nina fell asleep.

It seemed like only a few seconds later that Nina sat straight up in her sleeping bag. Something was wrong.

CHAPTER 8

A Bad Attack

Somebody was gasping and wheezing. Nina knew that sound well. Asthma!

Nina looked around and saw Greta was twisting in her sleeping bag, fighting to breathe.

Nina scrambled across the hay. She pulled
Greta out of her sleeping bag.

"Help!" cried Nina.

But no one came. In the dim light, Nina
could see Greta's eyes bulging with panic.
Nina held on to her tightly. Together they
slid down to the floor of the hay shed.

She half dragged and half carried Greta up
to the farmhouse.

Slamming the kitchen door behind them, Nina screamed, "Help! Help!" She knew that she needed to wake up Amy's mom and dad immediately.

Then Nina saw the telephone on the kitchen wall. She quickly dialed 911.

Amy's parents came out of their room. They looked confused.

"Could you tell the operator exactly how to get out to the farm?" asked Nina. She passed the phone to Amy's mom. "It's Greta. I think she's having a terrible asthma attack!"

Then Nina grabbed Mr. Bergner's arm.
She said, "Take Greta into the living room
and sit her on the couch. Can you put the
heat on? I'm going to see if my mom
packed an inhaler in my overnight bag.
Oh, yes, and please try to keep her calm."

Never before had Amy's parents seen a twelve-year-old take charge in an emergency. They didn't have any experience with asthma attacks, but Nina seemed to know what she was doing.

"Oh please, Mom," said Nina, searching wildly through the clothes in her bag. "I hope you were your usual careful self and packed an emergency allergy kit."

CHAPTER 9

Real Trouble

"OK, Greta, if I'm right, this inhaler should help you until the ambulance gets here," said Nina. She knelt down in front of Greta.

Nina placed the inhaler between Greta's lips and gave her two puffs.

"Now, we have to wait and see if you can breathe a bit better," said Nina.

But Greta was still gasping for air. Nina was starting to feel sick with worry.

Nina didn't really want Greta to use the inhaler again. She knew that you shouldn't use other people's medicine but . . . this was a life or death situation.

"Oh, where is the ambulance?" cried Nina.

Finally they heard a siren in the distance.

"You did a great job helping this girl," said one of the EMTs to the Bergners. "If she hadn't used an inhaler, she could have really been in trouble."

"All the credit goes to Nina Barco. She knew what to do. She kept her head and didn't panic," said Mr. Bergner.

"I've sort of been brought up on it," said Nina. She was relieved that the panic she'd started feeling had gone.

CHAPTER 10

A Local Hero

The news that Nina had saved Greta's life made the local newspaper's headlines. Nina immediately became famous in her new hometown.

When the EMTs were interviewed, they praised Nina's "quick thinking and confidence."

And Greta's parents nominated Nina for an award.

Nina's family was really proud of her. Her parents made her feel very special when they gave her a beautiful locket engraved with the date of Amy's party. It meant more to Nina than any award.

Greta had to stay in the hospital for several days, and Nina visited her often.

"So, how does it feel to be famous?" joked Greta, sitting up in her hospital bed. She was surrounded by flowers and toys. "Is it hard being recognized wherever you go?"

"Oh, yes, and the Heysville reporters—well, you've had a taste of them yourself, haven't you?" laughed Nina.

Greta smiled. "Yes, they talked to me, too."

Greta continued, "Actually, it's good I'm in the hospital. I'm learning all about what to do for my asthma. And it's good other kids in town are learning that having asthma isn't the end of the world."

"Right! You can still do most everything. You just have to remember your inhaler," agreed Nina. "I know this sounds awful, Greta, but in one way I'm glad about your asthma attack in the hay shed. It means I've found a best friend."

"And you need a best friend when you've just moved to a new town, don't you?" smiled Greta. "But I thought you were sick of people with asthma and allergies. I thought you wouldn't want to have anything to do with me."

"I've given up! I know that I'm always going to be surrounded by gaspers and scratchers," laughed Nina.

Meg Caraher

Meg started writing novels for fun when she was ten. At the age of seventeen, she won a scholarship as an exchange student in the United States. After her return to Australia, Meg attended the National Theatre School of Drama, in St. Kilda.

Meg's first children's book was published in 1995. She has won a poetry competition and received two short story awards. *Scritch! Scratch!* is her seventh book for children. Meg lives with her husband (Maurice), daughter (Stephanie), three pet chickens, and her Burmese cat (Binnie Noo Noo).

Pat Reynolds

Pat Reynolds has always loved painting and drawing, and she feels very lucky to have a job doing just what she loves—illustrating children's books. Sometimes she paints the illustrations in colored inks, and sometimes she uses colored tissue paper to make the pictures. For this book, she drew the pictures in graphite pencil—her favorite technique for black-and-white books.

When Pat finishes work for the day, she likes to go outside and plant little trees in the places where forests used to be.